12

SUGAR CREEK GANG

SCREAMS IN THE NIGHT

Paul Hutchens

MOODY PRESS
CHICAGO

© 1947, 1997 by
PAULINE HUTCHENS WILSON

Revised Edition, 1997

All Scripture quotations are taken from the *New American Standard Bible,* © 1960, 1962, 1963, 1968, 1971, 1972, 1973, 1975, 1977, and 1994 by The Lockman Foundation, and are used by permission.

Original Title: *Sugar Creek Gang Goes North*

ISBN: 0-8024-7016-5

7 9 10 8

Printed in the United States of America

PREFACE

Hi—from a member of the Sugar Creek Gang!

It's just that I don't know which one I am. When I was good, I was Little Jim. When I did bad things—well, sometimes I was Bill Collins or even mischievous Poetry.

You see, I am the daughter of Paul Hutchens, and I spent many an hour listening to him read his manuscript as far as he had written it that particular day. I went along to the north woods of Minnesota, to Colorado, and to the various other places he would go to find something different for the Gang to do.

Now the years have passed—more than fifty, actually. My father is in heaven, but the Gang goes on. All thirty-six books are still in print and now are being updated for today's readers with input from my five children, who also span the decades from the '50s to the '70s.

The real Sugar Creek is in Indiana, and my father and his six brothers were the original Gang. But the idea of the books and their ministry were and are the Lord's. It is He who keeps the Gang going.

PAULINE HUTCHENS WILSON

The *Sugar Creek Gang* Series:

1

I guess I never did get tired thinking about all the interesting and exciting things that happened to the Sugar Creek Gang when we went camping far up in the North. One of the happiest memories was of the time when Poetry, the barrel-shaped member of our gang, and I were lost out in the forest. While we were trying to get unlost we met a brown-faced Indian boy, whose name was Snow-in-the-Face, and his big brother, whose name was Eagle Eye.

Little Snow-in-the-Face was the cutest little Indian boy I had ever seen. In fact, he was the *first* one I'd ever seen up close. I kept thinking about him and wishing that the whole Sugar Creek Gang could go again up into that wonderful country that everybody calls the Paul Bunyan Playground and see how Snow-in-the-Face was getting along and how his big brother's Indian Sunday school was growing, which, as you know, they were having every Sunday in an old railroad coach they had taken into the forest and fixed up as a church.

I never had any idea that we would get to go back the very next summer. But here I am, telling you about how we happened to get to go, and how quick we started, and all the exciting things that happened on the way and after we got there—*especially* after we got there. Boy, oh, boy! It was fun—especially that night when we ran *ker-smack* into a kidnapper mystery, and some of us who were mixed up in it were scared almost half to death.

Imagine a very dark night with only enough moonlight to make things look spooky, and strange screaming sounds echoing through the forest and over the lake, and then finding a kidnapped girl all wrapped in an Indian blanket with a handkerchief stuffed into her mouth and—but that's getting ahead of the story, and I'd better not tell you how that happened until I get to it, because it might spoil the story for you. And I hope you won't start turning the pages of this book real fast and read the mystery first, because that wouldn't be fair.

Anyway, this is how we got to go.

Some of us from the Sugar Creek Gang were lying in the long mashed-down grass in a level place not far from where the hill goes down real steep to the spring at the bottom, where my dad is always sending me to get a pail of cold fresh water for us to drink at our house. We were all lying in different directions, talking and laughing and yawning and pretending to be sleepy. Some of us were tumbling around a little and making a nuisance of ourselves to each other. Most of us had long stems of bluegrass in our mouths and were chewing on the ends, and all of us were feeling great. I had my binoculars up to my eyes looking around at different things.

First I watched a red squirrel high up in a big sugar tree, lying flat and lazy on the top of a gray branch as though he was taking a two-o'clock-in-the-afternoon sunbath, which was what time of day it was that Saturday. I had been lying on my back looking up at the squirrel.

Then I rolled over and got onto my knees and focused the binoculars on Sugar Creek. Sugar Creek's face was lazy here, because it was a wide part of the creek, and the water moved very slowly, hardly moving, and was as quiet as Pass Lake had been up in Minnesota in the Paul Bunyan country on a very quiet day. There were little whitish patches of different-shaped specks of foam floating along on the brownish-blue water.

While I was looking at Sugar Creek with its wide, quiet face and dreaming about a big blue-water lake up North, I saw some V-shaped waves coming out across the creek from the opposite shore. The pointed end of the V was coming straight toward the spring and bringing the rest of the V along with it. I knew right away it was a muskrat swimming toward our side of the creek.

As I looked at the brownish muskrat through my binoculars, it seemed very close. I could see its pretty chestnut-brown fur. Its head was broad and sort of blunt, and I knew if I could have seen its tail it would have been about half as long as the muskrat, deeper than it was wide, and that it would have scales on it and only a few scattered hairs. I quickly grabbed a big rock and threw it as straight and hard as I could right toward the acute angle of the long moving V, which was still coming across the creek toward us.

And would you believe this? I'm not always such a good shot with a rock, but this time that rock went straight toward where the muskrat was headed. And by the time the rock and the muskrat got to the same place, the rock went *kerswishety-splash* right on the broad blunt head of the musquash, which is another and kind of fancy name for a muskrat.

Circus, the acrobat in our gang, was the only one who saw me do what I had done. He yelled out to me in a voice that sounded like a circus barker's voice, "Atta boy, Bill! Boy, oh, boy, that was a great shot! I couldn't have done any better myself!"

"Better than *what?*" nearly all the rest of the gang woke up and asked him at the same time.

"Bill killed an *Ondatra zibethica,*" Circus said, which is the Latin name for a muskrat. Circus's dad is a trapper, and Circus has a good animal book in his library. "Socked it in the head with a rock."

Everybody looked out toward Sugar Creek to the place where the rock had socked the *Ondatra* and where the two forks of the V were getting wider and wider, almost disappearing into nothing, the way waves do when they get old enough.

"Look at those waves!" Poetry said, meaning the new waves my big rock had started.

There was a widening circle going out from where it had struck.

"Reminds me of the waves on Pass Lake where we spent our vacation last summer," Poetry said. "Remember the ones we had a tilt-a-whirl ride on when Eagle Eye's boat upset and we got separated from it? If we hadn't had our life vests on we'd have been drowned because it was too far from the shore to swim!"

"Sure," Dragonfly piped up, "and that's the reason why every boy in the world who is in a boat on a lake or river ought to wear a life vest, or else there ought to be plenty of life preservers in the boat, just in case."

"Hey!" Little Jim piped up, squeaking in his mouselike voice. "Your On-onda-something-or-other has come to life away down the creek!"

And sure enough it had. Way down the creek, maybe fifty feet farther, there was another V moving along toward the Sugar Creek bridge, which meant I hadn't killed the musquash at all but only scared it. Maybe my rock hadn't even hit it, and it had ducked and swum under water the way *Ondatra zibethicas* do in Sugar Creek and as loons do in Pass Lake in northern Minnesota.

"I'm thirsty," Circus said. He jumped up from where he had been lying on his back with his feet propped up on a big hollow stump. That hollow stump was the same one his dad had slipped down inside once and had gotten bit by a black widow spider that had had her web inside.

Right away we were all scurrying down the steep hill to the spring and getting a drink of water apiece, either stooping down and drinking like cows or else using the paper cups that we kept in a little container we had put on the tree that leaned over the spring—in place of the old tin cup that we'd battered into a flat piece of tin and thrown into Sugar Creek.

All of a sudden, we heard a strange noise up at the top of the hill that sounded like somebody moving along through last year's dead leaves and at the same time talking or mumbling to himself about something.

"Sh!" Dragonfly said, shushing us, he being the one who nearly always heard or saw something before any of the rest of us did.

We all hushed, and then I heard a man's voice talking to himself or something up there at the top of the hill.

"Sh!" I said, and we all stopped whatever we had been doing and didn't move, all except Little Jim. He lost his balance and, to keep from falling the wrong direction—which was into a puddle of cold clean water on the other side of the spring—he had to step awkwardly in several places, jumping from one rock to another and using his pretty stick-candy-looking stick to help him.

We kept hushed for a minute, and the sound up at the top of the hill kept right on— leaves rasping and rustling and a man's voice mumbling something as though he was talking to himself.

All of us had our eyes on Big Jim, our leader. I was looking at his fuzzy mustache, which was like the down on a baby pigeon, wondering who was up on the hilltop, thinking about how I wished I could get a little fuzz on *my* upper lip, and wondering if I could make mine grow if I used some kind of cream on it or something, the way girls do when they want to look older than they are.

Big Jim looked around at the irregular circle of us and nodded to me, motioning with his thumb for me to follow him. He stopped all the rest of the gang from following. And the next minute I was creeping quietly up that steep incline behind Big Jim.

Little Jim also came along, because right at the last second Big Jim motioned to him that he could, as he had a hurt look in his eyes as if maybe nobody thought he was important because he was so little.

I had a trembling feeling inside of me. I just knew there was going to be a surprise at the top of that hill and maybe a mystery. Also, I felt proud that Big Jim had picked me out to go up with him, because he nearly always picks Circus, who is next biggest in the gang.

I didn't need to feel proud, though, because when I heard a little slithering noise behind me, I knew why Circus didn't get invited—he was halfway up a small sapling that grew near the spring. He was already almost high enough to see what was going on at the top of the hill. Circus was doing what he was always doing anyway, climbing trees most any time or all the time, looking like a monkey even when he wasn't up a tree. The only thing that kept him from hanging by his tail like a monkey was that he didn't have any tail, but he could hang by his legs anyway.

When we had almost reached the top, I felt Little Jim's small hand take hold of my arm tight, as if he was scared, because we could still hear somebody walking around and talking to himself.

Big Jim stopped us, and we all very slowly half crawled the rest of the way up. My heart was pounding like everything. I just knew there was going to be excitement at the top. And when you know there is going to be excitement, you can't wait for it but get excited right away.

"Listen!" Little Jim whispered to me. "He's pounding something."

"*Sh!*" Big Jim said to us, frowning fiercely, and we kept still.

What's going on up there? I wondered and wished I was a little farther up, but Big Jim had stopped us again so we could listen.

One, two, three—*pound, pound, pound.* There were nine or ten whacks with something on something, and then the pounding stopped, and we heard footsteps going away.

I looked back down the hill at the rest of the gang. Dragonfly's eyes were large and round, as they are when he is half scared or excited. Poetry had a scowl on his broad face, since he was the one who had a detectivelike mind and was maybe disappointed that Big Jim had made him stay at the bottom of the hill. Little red-haired Tom Till's freckled face looked very strange. He was stooped over, trying to pry a root loose out of the ground so that he'd be ready to throw it at somebody or something if he got a chance or if he had to. His face looked as if he was ready for some kind of fight and that he half hoped there might be one.

And if I had been down there at the bottom of the incline at the spring and somebody else had been looking down at me, he would have seen *another* red-haired, freckled-faced boy, whose hair was trying to stand up on end under his old straw hat and who wasn't much to look at but who had a fiery temper, which had to be watched all the time or it would explode on somebody or something.

Maybe, in case you've never read anything about the Sugar Creek Gang before, I'd better tell you that I am red-haired and freckled-faced and do have a fiery temper some of the time— and that my name is Bill Collins. I have a great mom and dad and a little baby sister, whose name is Charlotte Ann, and I'm the only boy in the Collins family.

I whirled around quickly from looking down the hill at the rest of the gang and from seeing Circus, who was up the elm sapling trying to see over the crest of the hill but probably couldn't. Big Jim had his finger up to his lips for all of us to keep still, which we did.

The pounding had stopped, and we could hear footsteps moving along in the woods, getting fainter and fainter.

Then Big Jim said to us, "He can't hear us now. His shoes are making so much noise in the leaves."

We hurried to the top and looked, and Little Jim whispered, "It's somebody wearing old overalls," which it was, and he was disappearing around the corner of the path that led from the spring down the creek, going toward the old sycamore tree and the swamp.

Big Jim gave us the signal, and all of us broke out of our very painful silence and were acting like ourselves again but wondering who on earth had been there and what he had been doing and why.

All of a sudden, Dragonfly, who had been looking around for shoe tracks with Poetry, let out a yell and said, "Hey, gang, come here! Here's a *letter* nailed onto the old Black Widow Stump!" which was the name we'd given the stump after Circus's dad had been bitten there.

We all made a rush to where Dragonfly's dragonflylike eyes were studying something on the stump, and then I was reading the envelope, which said, in very awkward old handwriting:

URGENT
To the Sugar Creek Gang
(Personal. Please open at once.)

2

I just stood there with all the rest of the members of the Sugar Creek Gang, staring at the envelope and the crazy old handwriting on it that said, "Personal. Please open at once."

Big Jim, the leader of our gang, reached out and tore the envelope off the nail that had been driven through the corner where the stamp would have been if there had been one. He handed it to me. "Read it out loud to all of us," he said.

I couldn't imagine what was on the inside. I didn't recognize the writing and couldn't even guess who had written it.

"Stand back, everybody," Big Jim ordered, "and let him have plenty of room."

"Yeah, let him have plenty of room. It might explode," Dragonfly said.

I tore open the envelope in a hurry, and this is what I read:

> Members of the Sugar Creek Gang—Big Jim, Little Jim, Poetry, Circus, Dragonfly, Bill Collins, and Tom Till—as soon as you can after reading this, make a beeline for Bumblebee Hill, climb through the barbed-wire fence at the top, and stop at the tombstone of Sarah Paddler in the old

abandoned cemetery. There you will find another letter giving you instructions what to do next. It is VERY IMPORTANT.

GUESS WHO

I read the letter out loud in a sort of trembling voice because I was a little scared. Then I looked around at different ones to see what they were thinking, but couldn't tell.

"What'll we do?" Little Jim piped up.

Little Tom Till swallowed hard as if he had taken too big a bite of something and was trying to swallow it. Then he sort of stuttered, "M-maybe a ghost wrote it."

I looked quickly at Dragonfly since he believes there is such a thing as a ghost, because his mother thinks there is, and right away he had a funny expression on his face. His dragonflylike eyes looked even larger than they were. "My mother told me to stay out of that cemetery," he said.

"Aw, fraidy-cat," Poetry said, "there isn't any such thing as a ghost. Besides, ghosts can't write."

"Oh, yes, they can," Dragonfly said. "I saw it in the newspaper once that a senator or somebody's speech was written by a ghostwriter and—"

"That's *crazy!*" Poetry said. "A ghostwriter is a person nobody knows, who writes something for somebody else, and nobody knows it. But it's a real person and not a ghost."

Poetry read an awful lot of the many books

his dad and mom were always buying for him, and he was as smart as anything.

Tom Till spoke up then and said, "A ghost wouldn't know that Bumblebee Hill had its name changed from Strawberry Hill to Bumblebee Hill, would it?"

And right away I was remembering that hill where the gang had had a fierce fight with a town gang, when Little Tom had still belonged to that other gang. We had all stirred up a bumblebees' nest and had gotten stung in different places, which had hurt worse than each other's fists had, and the fight had broken up. We'd given that hill a new name.

In that fight, as you may know, two red-haired boys had had a terrible battle. One of the red-haired, freckled-faced boys had licked the other one all to smithereens for a while—until I started fighting a little harder, and then I'd licked him even worse, all in the same fight.

Big Jim said, "A ghost probably couldn't spell our names. Anyway, let's get going to the old cemetery and see what happens."

With that, Circus was already on his way, running like a deer. All of us were right at his heels, running as fast as we could go.

Talking about spelling must have reminded Poetry of a poem. As you know, he was always learning new poems by heart and quoting them to us. He knew maybe a hundred of them, and you never knew when he was going to start one at the wrong time. He hardly ever got to finish one, though, because of the gang's stopping him or else it was too long to finish before we all thought of something we'd rather do than listen to his poem.

Anyway, while he and I were puffing along with the rest of the gang toward Bumblebee Hill, he started puffing out a new one I'd never heard before, and this is the way it went:

> "The teacher has no E Z time
> To teach his A B C's:
> It per C V rance takes sublime,
> And all his N R G's.
> In K C doesn't use the birch
> All kindness does S A,
> The scholars who X L at church,
> In school will 1/2 to pay . . ."

"Don't use the word *birch*," I panted to Poetry, and he panted back at me, "Why?"

"Because it reminds me of *beech*, and *beech* reminds me of a beech switch, which reminds me of a schoolteacher, and that reminds me of school, and—"

Poetry cut in on my sentence and said, "*Birch* reminds me of a birch tree away up North where we were on our camping trip once, and where I'd like to go again this year. In fact, it's getting so hot that I don't see how we can stand not going up there again."

I looked out of the corner of my right eye at him as we dashed along behind and beside and in front of the gang toward Bumblebee

18

Hill. I said, "I don't see why we have to stay where it is so hot all summer."

That started him off on his poem again, and he got another whole verse in before we reached the bottom of Bumblebee Hill and had to save most of our wind for climbing and not much for talking. This is the next verse, which he puffed out to me. The poem was still talking about a schoolteacher and went:

> "They can't C Y he makes them learn
> L S N and his rules.
> They C K chance to overturn,
> Preferring 2 B fools."

I found out later how to spell out the poem, when he showed it to me in his mother's old scrapbook. It was a clever poem, I thought.

Puff, puff, puff, up the hill we went, and at the cemetery we stopped. It was a real spooky place, all overgrown with weeds and chokecherry and blue vervain and mullein stalks. The blue vervain was one of the prettiest wildflowers in all Sugar Creek territory, but all the farmers called it a weed, and maybe it was. But up real close and under a magnifying glass, its flowers are very pretty.

Just as I was climbing through the fence beside Little Jim, holding two strands of barbed wire high enough apart for him to slither through and not get his nice new blue shirt caught, Little Jim, who is a sort of a dreamer and is always imagining what something or other looks like, said to me, "They look like upside-down candelabra, don't they?" Little Jim knew I liked flowers myself, because my mom liked them so well and always wanted me to pick some and set them in vases in different parts of our house.

"What looks like what?" Dragonfly said and sneezed, and I knew right away that he was allergic to something in the cemetery, as he was allergic to nearly everything in Sugar Creek in the summertime. And when people are allergic to things like that, they nearly always sneeze a lot.

Little Jim finished getting through without getting his shirt caught and said, "The flower spikes which branch off from the stem of the vervain look like upside-down candelabra."

I remembered that his mother, besides being the best pianist in all Sugar Creek territory, was maybe the prettiest mom of all the Sugar Creek Gang's moms. She also had all kinds of flowers in a special garden at their home, and she talked about flowers so much that Little Jim probably knew all the different kinds of words that people use when they talk about flowers.

Little Jim broke off a stalk of vervain, and I noticed that there was a purplish ring of small flowers at the very bottom of every one of the slender flower spikes, which is the way vervain do their flowering. They begin with a little purple ring at the bottom of the spike about the first of July, and the flowers keep on blooming all summer. The ring creeps up higher and higher until school starts about the first of September. Pretty soon the flowers get clear to the top, and then, like blue rings slipping off the ends of green fingers, they are all gone.

Well, soon there we all were, standing around in a sort of half circle, looking over each other's shoulders and between each other's heads, right in front of Old Man Paddler's dead wife's tall tombstone. Her name had been Sarah Paddler, and she had died a long time ago.

There were a couple of other tombstones there, too, for the old man's two boys. They had died about the same time many years ago, and now that kind old man, whom the Sugar Creek Gang loved so well, had maybe been using all the love that he'd had left over when his own boys died and was pouring it out on us *live* boys, instead of wasting it on a dog or a lot of other things.

Carved or chiseled on the tombstone was the figure of a hand with the forefinger pointing up toward the sky, and right below the hand were the words:

There Is Rest in Heaven.

Standing on a little ledge, and fastened onto the tombstone with tape, was an envelope like the one we had just found and had read down at the Black Widow Stump, and on it said:

To the Sugar Creek Gang
(Personal. Open at once.)

This time Big Jim took the envelope and handed it to Little Jim, who read it in his squeaky voice to all of us, and this is what it said:

The Sugar Creek Gang is on the right track;
Now turn right around and hurry right back—
Go straight to the old hollow sycamore tree,
And there, if you look, you will see what you see.

This time it wasn't signed "Guess Who," but the poetry sounded like Poetry's poetry, and I looked at him. He was busy studying the ground, though, to see if he could find any shoe tracks.

"Last one to the sycamore tree is a cow's tail," Circus said and was ready to make a dive for the cemetery fence.

Dragonfly got a funny look on his face, as if he was going to sneeze but wasn't quite sure whether he was or not. He looked toward the sun, which hurt his eyes a little, and that maybe made tears, which, with his face raised like that, tickled his nose on the inside. Anyway, he let out one of his favorite sneezes, which was half blocked like a football kick but went off to one side. Then he sneezed again three times fast, as if he couldn't help it, and said, "I'm allergic to something in this old graveyard. I'm allergic to ghosts."

Right away we were all dashing toward the barbed-wire fence, and all of us got through without tearing our clothes and went *zippety-zip-zip, dash, swerve, swish-swish-swish* toward the spring again. Then it was down the path that led along the top of the hill toward Sugar Creek bridge. And across the old north road. And up a steep bank. And down the path toward the old sycamore and the swamp—and also toward the entrance to the cave, which is a long cave, as you know, and the other end comes out in the basement of Old Man Paddler's log cabin back up in the hills.

"I'm thirsty," Poetry puffed beside me.

"So am I," I said, and right that second I remembered that when I'd gone to the spring in the first place, more than maybe an hour ago, I'd taken a pail from our milk house and was supposed to bring back a pail of sparkling cool water when I came home. "There isn't any hurry," Dad had told me, "but when you do come back, be *sure* to bring a pail of water."

"I will," I had said to him, and now as we raced past the spring, I remembered that the water pail was on a flat stone down at the bottom of the hill by the spring.

"Who do you suppose is writing all these notes?" I said to Poetry, forgetting the water again.

"Yeah, who do you suppose?" Poetry said from behind me.

"Come on, you guys!" Dragonfly yelled back to us from up ahead, and we all swished on.

It was quite a long run to the sycamore tree, but we got there quick and found Circus and Big Jim already inside the big long opening in its side, looking for the letter or whatever it was we were supposed to find. In a jiffy Circus had out a paper and was waving it around in the air for us to see.

When we gathered around, I saw that it was an envelope with our names on it, but this was an actual honest-to-goodness letter with a post-mark. When I got close enough to see, I saw it said "Pass Lake, Minnesota."

And something in my heart went flippety-flop. I just knew who the letter was from. For some reason I knew what was going to be inside. It was going to be a letter from the same friendly big man on whose Pass Lake property we'd had our camp last summer, and he was inviting us to come up again for a week or two or maybe more.

It certainly didn't take us long to find out that I was right, which I knew I was.

"It's from Santa Claus!" Dragonfly said.

Santa Claus was the name we'd given the man whom we'd liked so well on our camping trip and whose wife had made such good black-berry pies.

We all read the letter and felt so wonderful inside we wanted to yell and scream.

"Hurrah! Hurrah! Hurrah!"

There was one paragraph in the letter that bothered us, though, and it was:

Be sure, of course, to get your parents' consent, all of you, and be sure to bring along your fishing tackle. Fishing is good. Little Snow-in-the-Face will be eager to see you all. He has been very sick this past week and has been taken to the government hospital. Be sure to pray for him. His big brother, Eagle Eye, still has a Sunday school going here, but his mother and father are not yet believers on the Lord Jesus Christ, and that makes it hard for him. But Snow-in-the-Face is a very brave little Christian.

And right that second, we heard footsteps coming in our direction. Looking up, I saw a brown smiling face and a row of shining white teeth with one all-gold tooth right in front, and I knew it was Barry Boyland, Old Man Paddler's nephew, who had taken us to Pass Lake last year.

"Hi, gang!" he called to us, and we called back to him, "Hello, Barry." Then we all swarmed around him to tell him about the letter and to ask questions, all of us knowing that he was the one who had written the notes for us, just to make the last letter more mysterious and more of a surprise.

Well, it was time to go home and try to convince our parents that we all needed a vacation very badly. For some reason I wasn't sure my folks would say I could go.

3

How'll we do it?" I asked Poetry, as he and Dragonfly and I stopped at our gate to let them go on home and to let me go on in.

"How'll we do *what?*" Dragonfly wanted to know, and right away he sneezed at something or other, probably at some of the flowers in Mom's little flower bed around our mailbox.

Dragonfly reached into his hip pocket and pulled out his dad's big red handkerchief and grabbed his nose just in time to stop most of the next three sneezes, which came in one-two-three style, as fast as a boy pounding a nail with a hammer.

"How'll we convince our parents that we need a vacation?" Poetry said.

And Dragonfly said, "People take vacations when they're worn out from too much work."

"Overworking?" I said.

Dragonfly sneezed again and looked down at Mom's very pretty, happy-looking, different-colored gladiola in the half-moon flower bed around the mailbox.

"If you don't quit planting gladiola around here, I can't come over and play here anymore."

"Or work, either," Poetry said.

And I said, "Well, you guys better beat it. I've got to overwork a little."

I opened our gate, squeezed through it, and started on the run for our toolshed, where I found a nice clean hoe—which I'd cleaned myself the last time I'd used it—and soon I was out in the garden hoeing potatoes as hard as I could, getting hotter and hotter and sweating like everything. Sweat was running off my face, and I could feel it on my back too. With a little wind blowing across from the woods and Sugar Creek, I felt fine even in the hot sun. I certainly wasn't getting tired as fast as I thought I would. When a boy sweats at hard work and the wind blows a little, he feels better than when he just kind of lies around and tries to keep cool.

I wished Dad, who had gone somewhere for something, would hurry home and see me working hard. It was almost fun hoeing the potatoes, though it was hard not to stop at the end of each row and pick and eat a few luscious blackberries that grew there. In fact, I did stop a few times, which is maybe why I got to the end of each row quicker.

Once I got thirsty and went into the house for a drink of water, and Mom called out to the kitchen from the living room and said, "Is that you, Theodore?" which is Dad's first name.

"Nope, it's just me," I said.

"Come on in a minute, Bill. Somebody wants to see you."

"Who?" I said, wondering who it was and hoping it wasn't anybody I didn't know.

I peeked around the corner of the kitchen door and saw my lady Sunday school teacher. All of a sudden I felt good, although a little bashful because I was in my overalls and was probably very dusty and sweaty and maybe had my hair mussed up.

We said a few polite words to each other, and she said, "I brought you that book of Indian stories."

And right away I was thinking of little Snow-in-the-Face up North and wishing I could see him again.

I thanked her for the book, saying, "Well— thanks, that's great—I mean, thank you so very much," which was what I thought Mom would want me to say in the way I said it.

"Don't overwork," she said to me with a smile in her voice, and I said, "I will."

I was going out the kitchen door before I knew I'd said the wrong thing. She certainly was a good Sunday school teacher, though. She knew how to make a boy like her and also want to come back to Sunday school every Sunday.

Just as I was about to let the door shut behind me quietly the way I do when we have company, I heard the radio in the living room, and I knew that maybe Mom and my teacher had been listening when I came in and had turned it low for a while.

One of the things I heard was news about a little St. Paul, Minnesota, girl named Marie Ostberg having been kidnapped and a reward being offered by the father. Then I heard the announcer mention something that I thought was a wonderful idea. He said, "Duluth—the hay fever colony—will have thousands of new visitors this year because the heavy rains throughout the nation have made it the worst for pollen in many years. Thousands will be going north . . ."

That would give us *two* reasons that some of the gang ought to get to go, I thought—overwork and hay fever. Dragonfly had the hay fever, and if I worked extra hard, I might overwork, although it'd be easier to have hay fever if I could only get it.

While I was picking up the hoe to go back to the potatoes, I heard our car horn, and Dad was at the gate, waiting for me to come and open it. Was I ever glad I was hot and sweaty and that there were four or five long rows of potatoes already hoed, which Dad could see himself.

"Hi," I said to my reddish-brownish-mustached dad. And he just lifted one of his big farmer hands and saluted me as if I was an officer in the army and he only a private. I swung open the gate, and, seeing the gladiola by the mailbox, stopped and took three or four quick, deep sniffs at them, just as Dad swung the car inside and stopped beside the big plum tree by the graveled driveway.

Then I looked quickly at the sun, to see if I could sneeze, and I actually did, three times in quick succession, just as Dad turned off the motor and heard me do it.

"I hope you aren't going to catch cold," he said and looked at me suspiciously. "You boys go in swimming today?"

"The water was almost too hot," I said. "I never felt better in my life, only—" Right that second, something in my nose tickled again, and I sneezed and was glad of it. "Maybe I'm allergic to something down here."

"Down *where?*" Dad said, looking at me from under his heavy eyebrows, which I noticed weren't up anymore but were starting to drop a little in the middle, as though he was wondering, *What on earth?* and trying to figure me out, like a problem in arithmetic.

"I mean—" I started to answer and then decided maybe it was the wrong time to talk to Dad about what I wanted to talk to him about. So I said, "Well, I better get back to those potatoes. There are only two more rows."

"*Back* to them?" Dad said, astonished. "You mean . . ." He slid out of our long green car and looked toward the garden.

Even from where we were, you could see that somebody had been hoeing potatoes.

"Well, what do you know about *that?* That's wonderful! That's unusual! That's astonishing!" which I knew was some of Dad's friendly sarcasm, which he was always using on me, and I sort of liked it, because Dad and I were good friends even though he was my dad and I was his red-haired, freckled-faced overworked boy, who didn't have hay fever yet but was trying to get it.

Then I sneezed again, and Dad looked at me and said, "What's that grin on your face for?" and I said, "Is there a grin on my face?"

"There certainly is," he said.

I sighed and wished I could sneeze again, which for some reason I did, without even trying to or looking at the sun or smelling the gladiola or anything, and I got a quick hope that maybe I was actually going to get hay fever.

Dad took out a paper bag, which had something in it he'd probably bought somewhere in town, and banged the car door shut. Then he said, "Maybe you've been working too hard and been sweating, and—with the wind blowing—you need a dry shirt. Better come in the house and help your mother and Charlotte Ann and me eat this ice cream," which I did.

My Sunday school teacher helped also, since she was the reason Dad had hurried to town to get the ice cream in the first place.

Then Mom told me to gather the eggs, which I started out to do—and ran *ker-smack* into something very interesting.

I was up in our haymow looking for old Bent Comb's nest for her daily egg, which was always there if she laid one, although sometimes she missed a day.

"Well, what do you know?" I said to myself when I climbed up over the alfalfa to her corner. Old Bent Comb was still on the nest, and her pretty bent comb was hanging down over her left eye. She was sitting there as if she owned the whole haymow and who was I to be intruding?

"Hi, old Bent Comb!" I said. "How're you this afternoon? Got your egg laid yet?"

She didn't budge. She just squatted down lower with her wings all spread out, covering the whole nest.

"Where's your egg?" I said and reached out my hand toward her.

And *zip-zip-peck!* As quick as lightning her sharp bill pecked me on the hand and wrist. She wouldn't let me get near her without pecking, and when I tried to lift her off to see if she'd laid an egg today, she was mad as anything. She complained as if she was being mistreated and gave out a sad, disgruntled string of cluck-cluck-clucks at me and at the whole world. I let her stay.

Then I scooted down the ladder and ran *ker-whiz* to the house, stormed into our back door, and said, "Hey, Mom, old Bent Comb wants to set! What'll we do?—break her up or let her set?"

"For land's sake," Mom said to me, "don't knock the world off its hinges! *What? Old Bent Comb!*"

"Actually!" I said. "Up in the haymow!"

"We'll break her up," she said. "We can't have her hatching a nest of chickens up there."

"Couldn't we make her a nest down here— out by the grape arbor? Couldn't we put her in the new coop Dad and I made?"

"Better break her up," Mom said. "She's

one of our best laying hens. If we set her, she'll be busy all summer raising her family, and not an egg will we get."

"But we break her up every year, and she never has a family of her own," I said. "I think she'd look awfully proud and pretty strutting around the barnyard with a whole flock of little white chickens following her."

That's one of the prettiest sights a boy ever sees on a farm—a mother hen with a family of fuzzy-wuzzy little chickens behind and beside and in front of her, running quick whenever she clucks for them to come. Then they all gather around her and eat the different things she finds for them, such as small bugs, pieces of barnyard food, small grains of this or that, and just plain stuff.

"Well, maybe you're right," Mom said all of a sudden. "Let's set her. First, let's get her nest ready and select fifteen of the nicest leghorn eggs we can find and have them ready for her. Then you go get her and bring her down."

"She won't want to leave her nice warm nest up in the haymow," I said to Mom, looking up at her pretty, kind face under its blue sunbonnet.

"No, she won't," Mom said back to me, "but she'll do it if we work it right. Hens are very particular about moving from one nest to another. Maybe we'll have to shut her up in the coop."

Well, setting a hen was one of the most interesting things I liked to do around the farm. First, we took a nice brand-new chicken coop, which was just about as high as halfway between my knees and my belt. Then we scooped out a round hole a foot in diameter in the ground close to our grape arbor, making it only a few inches deep. We lined it with nice clean straw and then selected fifteen of the prettiest, cleanest white eggs we could find, which had been laid that very day by the other leghorn hens and which probably would hatch.

Then I ran *lickety-sizzle* to the barn, scooted up the ladder into the haymow, and in spite of Bent Comb's being very angry and not wanting to leave her nest, I got her under one arm and brought her down.

Soon Mom and I were ready to put her in the coop. I stooped down first and looked into the dark inside, and there were the prettiest, nicest, most beautiful fifteen eggs you ever saw, all side by side. The coop had a roof on it but no floor—only the ground with the straw nest on it.

I pushed Bent Comb very gently and in a friendly way up to the hole in the front of the coop and let her look in at the nestful of eggs. She had been clucking like everything and whining and complaining in a sad voice, which meant she wanted to be the mother of a whole flock of little chickens. But she was mad at me and didn't want to go in. She kept turning away from the hole in the coop, not even looking at the nice new nest.

So I said to her, "OK, Bent Comb, I'll take

you out and show you what will happen to you if you *don't* sit on those eggs."

I took her in both hands, holding her tight so she wouldn't squirm loose and get away. I walked with her to the chicken house and around behind it to where there was a peach tree under which we had a pen with chicken wire all around and on top. Inside were nine or a dozen of our best laying hens who had wanted to set but whom we decided to "break up" instead of letting them have their stubborn hen way.

There they were, all shut up by themselves. Some of them were walking around with their wings all spread out, clucking as if they wanted a bunch of little chickens to come and crawl under them. And they were cluck-cluck-clucking in a sad, whining tone of voice.

Over in one corner was a white egg, which meant that one of the hens had already given up wanting to "set" and was behaving herself again like a good laying hen. And I knew that as soon as we could decide which hen it was, we'd take her out and let her have her liberty again.

"See there," I said to Bent Comb. "Look at those lonesome old hens! They're clucking around just like you've been doing. Every one of them wanted a family of her own, and not one of them is going to get it! If you don't be good and go in that coop like we want you to, we'll have to shut you up in here and leave you for two whole weeks, which we do to all hens who want to set and we won't let 'em."

But Bent Comb wasn't interested at all. She absolutely refused to look, so I took her back to the coop. "I'm going to give you one more chance," I said. "I want you to go in there carefully, not breaking any of those eggs, and behave yourself."

Once more I got down on my knees, holding her carefully as though she was a very good friend—which she was—and so she could look in and see for herself what we wanted her to do.

Well sir, this time she must have decided to be good, because all of a sudden she quit struggling and looked in as if she'd made up her mind that it might be a good place for her for a while. Without my doing any pushing or anything, she very slowly started to creep inside the doorway toward the eggs. The next thing I knew she was on the nest, turning around and settling herself down and spreading her wings and covering every one of those fifteen eggs with her feathers.

I turned and yelled, "Mom! She's gone in! She's going to set!"

"Put the board over the hole for a while," Mom said, "so she can't get out. Let her stay until she feels at home, and then she'll go back every time we let her out for exercise and water and food."

I put the rectangular-shaped board over the door of Bent Comb's house and propped it shut with a brick, so she couldn't get out.

And so we "set" my favorite hen, old Bent Comb. In just three weeks there'd be a whole nestful of cheeping chicks and a very proud mama hen. I sat down for a minute on the roof of her house to rest. I was almost overworked, I started to think.

Then Dad yelled, "Hey, Bill, come on out here! We've got to get the rest of the chores done!"

So I started to the barn to help him, still thinking about the camping trip we'd all been invited to take and wondering if I would get to go.

"Don't you feel well?" Dad asked me as I was moving slowly around in the barn, doing different things.

"Kind of worn out," I said, and the dust which I'd been stirring up with a pitchfork over our corn elevator made me sneeze twice. "Maybe I've got hay fever," I said.

"That's the straw dust you're stirring up there," Dad answered.

"Stirring up?" I asked, but I knew he was right. You just couldn't fool Dad, I thought.

He stopped what he had been doing, which was something or other way up at the other end of the barn, and called to me, "Next week, we'll take you to the doctor and have him give you a test to see what makes you sneeze so much."

"Some people sneeze a lot because the rainy weather makes so many different kinds of flowers and weeds grow and so much pollen, maybe," I yelled back in a tired voice.

Dad ignored my educational remark and sent me up in the haymow to throw down some alfalfa for our brindle cow. While I was up there, I stirred up the dust in the hay and sneezed three or four times real loud.

Dad called up to me and said, "What's the matter, Bill? Are you hurt?"—which made me feel foolish.

The sun was shining through a crack in the barn. I peeped out, as I nearly always do when I'm up there, and looked around at different things such as the rows of newly hoed potatoes in the garden. I could hardly believe my eyes when I noticed that it was only *three* rows I'd hoed. It had seemed like at least seven.

Then I heard voices downstairs, and my heart almost jumped into my mouth. One of them was Barry Boyland's laughing voice. He and Dad were talking and saying they were glad to see each other.

I listened for all I was worth, and this is what I heard: "Well, Barry, we *have* to do something for him—he's getting the hay fever so badly. Maybe a trip North would be good for him."

And then Barry laughed the funniest laugh I'd heard in a long time. He said, "Sure, I understand. It's the same story wherever I go— the boys of the Sugar Creek Gang are all sneezing pretty bad—all except Dragonfly, who is better this year than last. But his parents said he could go too."

Then Dad and Barry laughed long and loud at each other as if it was funny or something.

But I didn't care at all. I was so tickled inside that a loud scream of happiness jumped up into my throat, and if I hadn't stopped it, I'd have yelled even louder than I do when I'm yelling for our baseball team. Oh boy, oh boy—another trip up North, with all the gang going along!

4

As you know, when we were thinking about going North, we didn't have any idea we'd run into an exciting and dangerous mystery. But when a gang of boys gets together on a camping trip in the wild North, something is nearly always bound to happen.

On the way we went through a city that advertised itself as the "Capital of the Paul Bunyan Playground." Paul Bunyan is the mythical lumberman of the North and was supposed to have been very big, like the giant in "Jack and the Beanstalk," which is a fairy story every boy ought to know—only instead of Paul Bunyan's being a *bad* giant, he was a good one and was always doing kind things for people.

We stopped to get some gas for Barry Boyland's station wagon, right across from a tourist camp called "Green Gables," and Little Jim gasped and said, "Look! Who and what is that?"

I looked out at what he was looking at and saw a huge statue of a man with a beard and a mustache, standing with one hand upraised and the other on the back of a statue of a great blue cow.

Poetry spoke up and said, "That's Paul and Babe."

"Paul and Babe *who?*" Dragonfly wanted to know.

And Poetry, who, as I've told you, had a lot of books in his library, all of a sudden reached down into the backpack he had with him and pulled out a book and said, "That's Paul Bunyan and his big blue ox, whose name is Babe. It was the blue ox whose footprints were so large that when it walked around they sank deep into the ground, and everywhere it went it left big holes. Then when it rained, the rainwater filled up the holes, and that made all the eleven thousand great big blue-water lakes in Minnesota."

Little Jim, who likes fairy stories and legends, grinned and said, "What made the water blue then? How come?" You see, nearly all the water in the hundred lakes we'd already seen on our trip was as blue as the hair ribbon that Circus's sister wore to school at Sugar Creek.

"What made the lakes blue?" asked Poetry with a question mark in his voice. He puckered his wide forehead and said, "Blue—oh, *that!*" He thumbed his way through the Paul Bunyan book quickly to see if there was anything in the book to explain it, but there wasn't. So he said, "Old Babe, the ox, was blue, you know. One day when he was out swimming in the headwaters of the Mississippi, the blue began to come off, and pretty soon the Mississippi, which flows through a lot of lakes up here, was all blue. The water flowed all around from lake to lake and pretty soon the lakes' waters were all blue too!"

Well, it was as good an untrue story as any of the rest of the exaggerated ones in the Paul Bunyan book, so we added it to the list and decided to tell it to our folks when we got back to Sugar Creek.

Soon we were driving on, straight through the pretty little modern-looking city, where there were lots of people walking the streets in vacation clothes.

We passed a tourist information place on the right side of the road, where there was a tall cement water tower that was shaped exactly like my dad's long six-battery flashlight back home. It was a lot larger at the top than the bottom. Little Jim squinted his blue eyes up at it as though he was thinking about something.

Then we went on, and Poetry read to us different crazy things the mythical Paul Bunyan was supposed to have done. He had been such a big baby that when he was born it took six large storks to carry him to his parents. Paul's pet mosquitoes dug the wells up here where we were. And his soup bowl was so large it was like a lake, and the cook had to use a boat to get across it. His pancake griddle was so big that they greased it by tying greasy griddle cakes on the bottom of some men's shoes, and they skated around over its surface to grease it for Paul. Stories like that.

Little Jim surprised us all of a sudden by saying, "Anybody want to hear how all the people decided to move up into this country and stay here? How Paul Bunyan and I working together got them to come when nobody wanted to?"

"How?" Dragonfly wanted to know. "And what do you mean, you and Paul Bunyan worked it? Paul used to live here long before you were born. You never even saw him!"

"Oh, I didn't, didn't I?" Little Jim said and had a very mischievous grin on his innocent face. "Want to hear the story?"

"Sure," Poetry and I said.

"No," Dragonfly said.

Little Jim said, "All right, I won't. Anyway, it's too important a story to tell to such a small, unappreciative audience." He sighed as if he was sleepy and curled up with his head on my lap and sighed again. Almost before I knew it, he was actually asleep.

It felt good having Little Jim lying with his head in my lap. He was my almost best friend, except Poetry, and also was a really wonderful guy and the best Christian in the whole Sugar Creek Gang. He was always thinking and saying important things about the Bible and heaven and the One who had made the world—and also about His Son who had come to this world once and died on a cross made out of a tree, just to save anybody who would repent of his sins and believe on Him.

I looked down at that curly head and thought of Sugar Creek and my parents and little Charlotte Ann and was lonesome for a minute. Then pretty soon I was sleepy myself, and the flying tires of the station wagon sort of sang me to sleep too. Once I half woke up because Little Jim wiggled and I heard him mumbling something. I was too sleepy to listen, but it sounded as if he thought he was at home getting ready to crawl into bed.

I bent my ear down a little and listened, and I heard some pretty words. They were,

> "Now I lay me down to sleep.
> I pray the Lord my soul to keep.
> If I should die before I wake,
> I pray the Lord my soul to take."

I'd heard the poem before —in fact my folks had taught it to me, and, when I was smaller, I'd said it at night myself.

Little Jim said something else I couldn't quite make out, but it sounded like this: "Please also bless little Snow-in-the-Face and help him to get well . . ."

Then I felt Little Jim's shoulder relax against my stomach, and I knew he was sound asleep. In another jiffy I was asleep myself.

When I woke up, we were still flying along with Barry at the wheel, and most of us were lying back, getting a great afternoon nap. It was wonderful to ride along that fast and also wonderful to see all the things we saw as the road wound itself around and around like the barefoot-boy paths through the woods along Sugar Creek.

At the town of Pass Lake most of us got out, stretched ourselves, bought postcards at a drugstore, and sent them to our folks. I sent a cartoon card that showed some men climbing a tree. Some big fish were at the bottom, looking up the way hungry bears look at boys.

I wrote to my folks, "Pretty soon we'll be making camp," which we did about a quarter of a mile from the place we'd been the year before on Santa's lakefront property. Santa, as you know, is the big laughing man who likes kids almost as much as Old Man Paddler does.

"Where's *Mrs.* Santa?" Poetry asked, maybe remembering the blackberry pie she'd given us and maybe missing her very friendly and extra special giggle, which we'd all liked to hear so well. I had looked forward to seeing her laugh with her eyes as well as hearing her laugh with her birdlike voice.

Santa was sitting in his big white boat, which was beached near where we were making camp, and was helping Tom Till get his fishing pole and line ready for a fishing trip in the morning. He said to Poetry, "She's gone to California, but she'll be back early next week, before you boys will have to go back to Sugar Creek."

Well, it was almost time for the sun to go down, and we would have to get busy pitching our tents. Barry called to us from the station wagon, which was parked close by, "Hey, gang! Let's get the tents up! You, Bill! Poetry! Tom!"

We all came running and pretty soon were working like Boy Scouts, doing what is called "making camp." Barry'd picked a site not far from the lake and also not too far from a woodpile, so that a gang of boys who were lazy only when there was work to do wouldn't have to carry wood too far. Also he chose a place where there wouldn't be too much shade. It wouldn't be too damp, and we would have sunshine every day if there was any.

"Why don't we put the tents under this big tree right here?" Circus asked.

And Barry said, looking up at the tree, "See that great big half-dead limb there?"

Dragonfly looked up and saw it. "Sure, what of it?"

Little Jim said, "The wind might blow some night," and then he turned and ran to where Big Jim was, who with his jackknife was cutting green sticks of different sizes to help us make what Barry called an outdoor kitchen. He said it was going to be like the kind the Chippewa Indians used to use.

All of us were either giving or obeying orders, and soon our tents were up, and the outdoor kitchen was nearly finished.

"OK, you guys—you and Poetry," Barry ordered Poetry and me, "roll up two of those big round rocks over there, get a couple of forked sticks, and push them right into the fire."

We already had a roaring fire going in a place where it was safe to have one. No boy or anybody else ought to start a fire in any forest anytime unless it is in a place where there is supposed to be one and where it can't spread, or a whole forest might get burned up.

"What for?" I said, as Poetry and I, grunting, each pushed a round rock up as close to the hot fire as we could. Then we pushed them the rest of the way with sticks so that we wouldn't get burned.

"Wait and see," Barry said, and we did but kept wondering, *Why on earth?*

We brought two other rocks also, while the rest of the gang helped put up the tents and made things ready for our first night's sleep. I had a tingling feeling inside of me and just knew we were going to have the most wonderful time of our lives.

It didn't take us long to get supper over, which we cooked on a little two-burner pressure gas stove that Barry had brought along. He didn't want us to take time to cook in real Indian style, which we would most of the time.

"Ouch!" we said to each other and all of a sudden started slapping at mosquitoes.

"Here—rub this on," Barry said, "and be careful not to get any too near your eyes and lips."

He handed us a couple of bottles of mosquito lotion, and we smeared our bare hands and ankles and necks and ears and faces with the sickening sweet-smelling stuff. And right away it was just as if there wasn't a mosquito in the world.

Santa came over, and we all sat around the campfire. While the pretty sparks and flames played above the bed of coals and the four large round rocks in the middle of it, Barry told us a thrilling and very interesting Bible story, which maybe I ought to tell you here myself, because it was one of the best stories a real red-blooded gang of boys ever heard.

All of us were on blankets in a sort of half circle around the campfire, some of us leaning up against each other. Right that minute I was against Poetry.

"Get over," Poetry said to me. "Don't crowd so close."

"I'm trying to get warm," I said. "It's cold. I'm using you for a windbreak."

And Circus said to Poetry, "You're a good windbreak when it's cold, and when it's hot we lie behind you in the shade."

Poetry, as you know, is not small. Most of us giggled—except Poetry.

"It happened like this . . ." Barry began.

I noticed that Little Jim reached into his vest pocket and pulled out his New Testament to look up the place where Barry was reading the story. I did the same. So did most of the gang, except for Tom Till, who had forgotten to bring his.

I looked at Tom, and he swallowed as though he was embarrassed, so I reached out mine to him, and he sort of looked on, although I knew he couldn't see very well and wasn't good at reading the Bible anyway. Besides it was more interesting to watch Barry's brown face in the firelight when he talked.

It was one of my very favorite Bible stories and was about some fishermen who lived near a great blue-water lake that was thirteen miles long and seven miles wide and had thousands of fish in it. Two brothers named Peter and Andrew were fishing, not with poles but with nets, and two other brothers, whose names were James and John and whose dad's name was Zebedee, were using another boat. I was feeling sorry for the double brothers, because they hadn't caught any fish, and I was wondering what their moms would say when they got home.

Then Barry started talking about a big crowd of people coming along and listening to Someone tell wonderful stories and also tell them about the Father in heaven and how to live right and things like that. The crowd got so close to the speaker that He might have been crowded into the water.

He turned and asked Peter to let Him borrow his boat, so that He could get into it and push out from shore a little. Then He could talk to the crowd and not get trampled on, and also the crowd would be able to see Him.

It was a bright idea, I thought. I wished I had been there, because if it was wonderful to hear our minister at Sugar Creek tell about Him in his very interesting sermons, it would have been even more wonderful to have been beside that pretty blue lake that day and listening to the Savior right while He was talking.

Pretty soon the speaker's sermon was over, Barry said, and then, just as if He wanted to pay Peter for being so courteous as to let Him make a pulpit out of his boat, He told Peter to shove the boat into the deep water and let down the nets for some fish.

Well, Peter didn't want to do it. He said he had been fishing around there all night and hadn't caught anything, and he might have wondered, *Why do it again and make a fool of myself?*

"But," said Barry—and even though he was smiling, his face was very serious—"it is better to obey the Lord, boys—even if it does seem foolish to the world for you to do it—than to *disobey* Him. Besides, He has a right to give us orders, since He is the Son of God."

He kept on talking, but for a minute I looked at Circus, who I noticed had his fists doubled up and was lying on his stomach and his elbows, looking up and across the fire at Barry. Also he had his chin resting on his doubled-up fists, and the muscles of his jaw were working. I thought maybe he was imagining himself to be Peter, and his thoughts were right out in that pretty lake, and he was seeing the whole thing with his mind's eye the way I was.

When my thoughts got back to Barry again, he was farther along in the story to where the net was suddenly jammed full of big bouncing, swishing, lunging, splashing fish, and Peter and Andrew had to have help to pull the net in. And the big strong net began to break in places, and some of the fish were getting away! So Peter let out a yell for James and John to bring their boat. They did, quick, and the boats soon were so filled with fish that both started to sink.

That scared Peter, for all of a sudden Peter realized that the Man he'd been listening to was more than a man. He was also the Lord. He suddenly realized, too, what a terrible sinner he was, and he forgot all about the bouncing, swishing, lunging, splashing fish and dropped down on his knees and cried, "Go away from me, Lord, for I am a sinful man, O Lord!" He was so ashamed of himself for being sinful that he didn't think he was good enough to be anywhere near the Lord.

But Jesus had done all this on purpose—to get Peter to believe in Him—and He told him not to be afraid any longer. He said, "Do not fear, from now on you will be catching men."

When Barry said that, Circus's bright eyes lit up, and he interrupted the story to say, "What'd He mean by that?"

Before Barry could answer, Little Tom Till surprised us all by cutting in and saying across the crackling fire to Circus, "He meant, 'Don't be scared. From now on you'll be what our Sugar Creek minister calls a *soul winner*.'"

It was a wonderful true story, and for some reason I had the happiest feeling inside. I not only wished all of a sudden that I had been there and had maybe been Peter or Andrew or one of Zebedee's two boys, but I felt also that maybe the most important thing in the world was to be a soul winner, or a fisher of men.

Well, Barry's story was done, and the sky above the lake toward where the sun had gone down reminded me of the reddish, purplish, and also yellowish spread-out feathers of a terribly big fantail pigeon.

5

I was sitting there on a small log, looking at the extra beautiful sky over the top of our campfire, thinking about how the rays of the sun shooting up looked like a lady's many-colored unfolded fan or the tail of a fantail pigeon, when Barry said, "One of the sporting clubs up here is offering a prize for the best original Paul Bunyan story. Here's a chance for you boys to stretch your imaginations a little."

Since it seemed a good idea, we decided to see who of us could make up the best one. So after we'd listened to Barry tell us that Bible story about something that had *really* happened on Galilee Lake once, we all took turns telling made-up stories.

We were all racking our brains to see if we could think of something about Paul Bunyan that nobody had ever thought of before, which Barry might decide was good enough to write about and send in to the contest.

We made up different things, such as:

One time Paul Bunyan gave a wintertime party in a terribly big recreational center in Bemidji, and so many people answered his invitation and came that there wasn't any place to hang their fur coats and other heavy clothes.

So Paul went out and blew on his horn, and

hundreds of huge antlered deer came running in from all directions. Paul stood them up all around the outer wall of the building, each one of them facing the center, and the people hung their fur coats and other kinds of different-colored coats on the antlers, using them for what is called "costumers." Those deer stood there patiently, without moving, with their kind eyes watching the guests.

Everything was going fine until somebody opened all the doors to let in some fresh air. All of a sudden, old Babe, the blue ox, came in and started lumbering around looking for Paul. He stamped his hoofs and snorted like a mad bull, and the people got scared and excited, and the women started screaming, and that scared the hundreds of deer, and they bolted for the doors in a mad and wild scramble. Since the doors all around them were open, they took all the coats with them.

That was Big Jim's story, and when he told it I remembered that he always got very good grades in English in the Sugar Creek School.

Dragonfly said Paul Bunyan got hay fever so bad and sneezed so hard and so many times in succession that it blew a whole forest over.

Poetry said Paul Bunyan ate so many blackberry pies and got so big that, when he went in swimming in Leech Lake and splashed around a lot, water splashed out of the lake for hundreds of miles around. It made a thousand *new* lakes so that the ten thousand lakes that Minnesota had at first were changed to eleven thousand.

Circus said that the day Paul ate Poetry's blackberry pies he had to have toothpicks to pick the seeds out from between his teeth, so he cut down some Norway pines with his jack-knife, which was seven feet long, and used them for toothpicks.

Dragonfly looked at me and my red hair with a mischievous look in his dragonflylike eyes and told another story real quick: Paul's long hair was so red that, when he was asleep one windy day, the Indians saw it blowing in the wind and thought it was a forest fire. They threw water all over him, and ever since then all red-haired people have been all wet.

Well, that was supposed to be funny, and most everybody around the campfire thought it was and laughed hard. But it wasn't funny. For a minute I was almost mad but decided it would be a waste of good temper to spoil what the others thought funny. Besides, my dad says any boy who wants to get along with people can't afford to always be taking offense.

I couldn't think of anything about Paul Bunyan that would help me get even with Drag-onfly, so I let Little Jim tell his story, and then we didn't have time for mine, because it was time to go to bed.

I watched Little Jim's small friendly face in the firelight and in the light of the afterglow of the sun, which had already gone to bed, and he looked so innocent that you couldn't tell whether he was thinking or not. But it was fun to listen to him, because his mouselike voice squeaked out the strangest story, which really sounded good.

He began: "Well, when Paul and I were up here in this pretty country of many lakes, we got awful lonesome and wished there were some other people living here. We stayed down where Brainerd is now, and Paul would carry me around in his vest pocket and tell me stories and complain about how lonesome he was."

It sounded as if Little Jim was going to have a real good story, so I listened, and sure enough it was. That little innocent-faced guy said Paul Bunyan finally got so lonesome that he took his long brown flashlight and some different-colored cellophane and stood the flashlight—which was two hundred feet long—up on the ground, and built a wooden platform around it right at the place where the switch was.

Every night Little Jim sat on that platform of the two-hundred-feet-tall flashlight and turned that light on and off and on and off. Paul would stand beside the flashlight and slide different-colored pieces of cellophane paper across the top of the flashlight, and the whole sky was all lit up in many different colors every night, changing just like the beautiful northern lights. (I thought that maybe the sky above the lake had made Little Jim think about the different colors.)

In a week or so, people from Iowa, Missouri, Tennessee, and all the Southern states began to come up North to see what they thought were the northern lights. They liked the country so well they decided to stay and build their homes, which they did, and so the town of Brainerd was founded. And then Paul just left his flashlight standing, and the people took the big batteries out and used it for a water tower, where it still stands in downtown Brainerd.

Well, it was a cute idea, and I wished I could think of something good, but I couldn't, so we broke up our campfire circle.

Santa stood and yawned and stretched his big self into a straightened-up posture. He looked straight at Tom Till and said, "How about a spin on the lake with my new outboard motor, Tom?"

I remembered that Santa and Mrs. Santa didn't have any children of their own, and that last year he had liked Tom so well and had also been the one who had shown Tom how to become a Christian. I knew too that Tom's dad was an unbeliever and was hardly ever kind to him, and maybe Tom was hungry for some grown-up person to like him. So I felt happy inside that Tom was going to get a fast boat ride, although I wanted to go along more than anything.

"You, too, Bill—and Poetry, if you like," Santa said, "if you can spare them awhile, Barry. I'll take the rest of the gang tomorrow. This new motor needs breaking in, you know."

Well, it was all right with Barry, and it certainly was all right with me, so away we four went toward the sandy shore where Santa's big white boat was beached. Each of us took our life preserver vest and put it on before getting into the boat.

The lake looked wonderful, having as many colors as the sky itself, which meant that a lake got its color from the sky, I thought. I said to Poetry, "Looks like old Babe, the ox, must have changed his colors like a chameleon and taken a swim out here while we were telling stories."

And Poetry surprised me by yelling, "Great, Bill. That's wonderful! Hey, you guys back there! Bill's got a good story!"

Well, it made me feel half proud of myself to have Poetry yell that to the gang, and I liked Poetry a lot for a minute. That was one of the reasons I liked him anyway—he was always making another person feel he was worth something.

It certainly felt fine to sit in the prow of Santa's boat, with Tom Till and Poetry in the middle and Santa himself in the stern, and go roaring out across the lake. In the afterglow of the sunset the lake was pretty, and without much wind it was as smooth as Mom's mirror in our living room at home. I was wishing Dad and Mom were there to see things. But I wouldn't want them to *stay*, because I wanted to have some real exciting adventures to tell them about when we got home.

Pretty soon our boat cut a wide circle

around the end of a neck of land, and we went roaring down the other side maybe a hundred feet from shore. It was still a little light on the lake, but the pine trees on the shore looked dark, and it was getting dark fast.

I was wondering if we would run into any exciting adventures up here in the North when Poetry said, "Look, Bill! Right there's where our boat upset last year and tossed us out. And right there's where I hooked that big northern pike."

I remembered. I yelled back and said so and then went on thinking—wishing we'd have some kind of scary excitement as well as a lot of fun camping.

I watched the widening waves that spread out behind us like a great V. I felt fine and happy. For some reason I liked everybody. Also I was remembering the Bible story Barry had told and how Peter was afraid to have the Lord anywhere near him because he was a sinner. I began to feel that God was real close to all of us, and I wasn't a bit scared of Him, because I knew that He had washed all my sins away, which our Sugar Creek minister and Little Jim say is what He does for a boy—or anybody—who will really let Him.

Just then Poetry yelled to me, "Penny for your thoughts, Bill!"

I jumped and looked at him and said, "Look at that reddish sky, will you?"

Poetry looked and said, "Kind of pretty, isn't it?"

6

We docked and went into Santa's log cabin with him. It was cozy inside. First, he lit two old-fashioned kerosene lamps. Then, because it might get cold pretty soon, we helped him start a fire in his small woodstove in a corner. Tom pumped a pail of water from the pitcher pump inside the cabin. Santa even had an ice-box, and twin beds in another small room. In a tiny room way in the back there was a bathtub and beside it a very old-fashioned trunk that for some reason made me think of Robinson Crusoe and buried treasure.

I wished harder than ever that we would run into a mystery up here in the North. I was all tingling inside, wanting one so bad. Of course, I wouldn't want the kind that would scare a boy half to death, like the ones that *sometimes* happened to the Sugar Creek Gang. But I wanted an ordinary mystery anyway.

Soon it would be time to go back to camp and get to sleep. I was wondering how we could keep warm in our cold tents when there wouldn't be any fires inside and we didn't have any heaters. Of course I knew I'd be pretty warm myself after I'd crawled into my sleeping bag. But it'd be cold to get undressed before getting into my pajamas.

Santa showed us different things in his cottage, such as a large mounted fish on the wall, which Mrs. Santa had caught, and also a great bearskin rug on the floor, which had a fierce bear's head with a wide-open red mouth on one end of it. Also there was a snakeskin on the wall, which a missionary in Africa had sent him.

When it was time to go home, Poetry looked at Santa's woodbox and said all of a sudden, "You need a load of wood—better let Bill carry one in for you."

"Fine," I said. "I'll hold the flashlight for you." I took a flashlight off the table and started toward the door with Poetry right after me.

When we were outside, we looked back through the window of the pretty little cabin at Santa and Tom standing by the fire warming themselves, and all of a sudden Poetry said, "I wish Tom had a dad like—I wish Santa was Tom's dad."

I thought of old hook-nosed John Till at Sugar Creek and knew that at that very minute he was probably standing at the bar in a beer joint and that maybe Tom's mother was not even going to have enough money to buy groceries for the family the rest of that week.

At the long woodpile, Poetry and I stopped. He said, "*Sh!* Turn off the light. I heard something."

I snapped off the flashlight, peered out into the dark, and listened. "It's a crazy loon," I said, when one of those diving birds away out on the dark lake somewhere let out a long-tailed quavering cry, which came echoing across to where we were. Right away another loon, closer to the shore, answered him.

And then my hair started to stand up on end, because I heard another sound almost like that of a loon, but it wasn't coming from that lake. It sounded like a little girl crying, and it came from over in the direction of the boathouse where Santa kept his boat in the winter and his tools and oars and things in the summer.

Then I heard the sound again, plain as day, a faint cry like a loon that somebody was trying to smother, maybe with his fingers on its throat.

Poetry's hand was tightening on my shoulder. His face was close to my neck, and I could hear and feel him breathing. "Over there," he whispered huskily, "close to the boathouse. Down!" He drew me down beside him, both of us hiding behind the woodpile.

Before I ducked, though, I looked in the direction of the boathouse. It was up against the edge of a steep hill, and I saw a tiny glow as if somebody had drawn on a cigarette or cigar and it had made a glow in the dark.

I knew it couldn't be any of our camping party smoking because none of us smoked, not even Barry.

Then I heard the boathouse door creaking on its hinges, and I knew I was beginning to be scared.

"It's a man smoking," Poetry hissed in my ear.

But I didn't want to believe it. "Maybe it was

a lightning bug," I said. There were several of them flashing their spooky little lamps on and off out near Santa's boat.

"Lightning bugs' lights are a yellowish green," Poetry said, "and that was a reddish glow."

I knew he was right but hoped, in spite of wanting a mystery, that whatever it was wasn't some criminal. Then I heard what sounded like a stifled cry again, and I knew it wasn't any loon. I said to Poetry, "Maybe it's a loon's echo."

I had the flashlight in my hand and without thinking, just doing what I wanted to, I shot its long white beam straight toward the boathouse, up against the hill.

Poetry reached out a hand and grabbed my arm and smothered the light against his side, but not before I saw what I saw, which was a dark shadow of something dart behind the boathouse.

"Don't scare whatever it is," Poetry said. "Give me time to think what to do." Poetry, as you know, is the one of our gang who wanted to be a detective and knew more about being one than any of the rest of us.

We both ducked behind the woodpile again and knelt on a pile of sawdust, which might have been left there when somebody cut the wood with a buzz saw. Even with a scary mystery just around the corner, Poetry quoted something he had memorized, which was:

"If a wood saw would saw wood,
How much wood would the wood saw saw
If the wood saw would saw wood?"

"I thought you wanted to think," I said to him.

"I am," he said. "I think best when I have what books call a 'poetic muse.' Did you notice what I noticed?" he asked me.

"What?" I said.

And he answered, "That the boathouse has had a new coat of paint since we were here last year."

"I saw a shadow move," I answered him. I was trembling inside and listening toward the boathouse.

We kept on listening but didn't hear a thing, so we decided to turn the flashlight on the boathouse again. It was painted a nice, pretty green color. It even looked as if it had *just* been painted.

"Smell the paint?" Poetry said, and I did— for the first time.

That green boathouse had its door closed and looked as innocent as Little Jim's face. There wasn't a sound of any kind. A lonely loon let out a wavering wail from across the lake, and another one answered him from close to the shore, not far from the dock where we had just left Santa's boat. But there wasn't another sound anywhere.

"What about the door creaking on its hinges?" I said.

"Just remember it when we start questioning the suspect later on," Poetry said, and his voice was as calm as if he was actually a detective. But his hand was on my arm, and I could feel it trembling a little.

We loaded up our arms with wood as quick as we could and started toward the cottage.

We were both shaking when we got inside, but we'd made up our minds to keep quiet so as not to scare Tom Till. Also, if we were only imagining things because we wanted a mystery to solve, and if there really wasn't any, we didn't want to seem silly to anybody except ourselves, which wouldn't be so bad.

We unloaded our two armloads of wood into the big woodbox in the corner beside the stove and then looked around. I saw on the table a copy of a Minneapolis newspaper and on the front page a big headline that said, "Fear Ostberg Kidnapper Hiding in Chippewa Forest."

I stared and stared at the headline and sidled quickly over to the table. In the light of the flashlight—the kerosene lamp wasn't bright enough—I read the whole story. I was remembering the radio program I'd heard back in our house at Sugar Creek—about a little girl being kidnapped in St. Paul.

Poetry came over, and we read the newspaper article together while Santa and Tom Till were opening the icebox and getting out some bottles of pop. Poetry's hand was gripping my arm so tight that it hurt, but I didn't say a word.

I was concentrating on the news story of the little girl who had been taken from her home and hadn't been found yet. I was thinking that the kidnapper, whoever he was, might be right that minute out there in Santa's boathouse, and the Ostberg girl too. The father of the little golden-haired girl had already paid the ransom money of $25,000, but the kidnapper hadn't left the girl where he'd promised to.

7

It was hard to keep still while we were drinking our pop from Santa's icebox. In fact, I couldn't, so I said, "You been doing some painting around here, Santa? I smell fresh paint outdoors."

Santa set down his bottle of orange pop on the table and swallowed and said, "The boathouse? Yes, I gave it a new coat yesterday. I've been doing a little work inside the boathouse too —doing it up in green and white. I plan to use it for a den for my fishing tackle and guns, and a place to write. And when I have company, it'll do for a guest house—or a sleeping room, anyway."

Then Santa got an odd look on his face, straightened up, and said, "What do you know? I just remembered I forgot to lock the boathouse door."

Tom Till spoke up and asked, "Do the Indians steal things up here when you leave the doors unlocked?"

And Santa answered and said something everybody ought to know: "There are *white* people up here who do. We have very little trouble with the Indians themselves. They like to be trusted, and if they think you've locked the door especially because of them, they resent it.

Of course, there are Indians and Indians, as there are white men and white men. A man isn't a thief because he's an Indian or of any other race but because he has a sinful nature, which all men do have. A man decides for himself whether he is going to steal or not. It doesn't matter what the color of his face is, if he has a sinful heart."

Santa stretched himself and started toward the door.

I was wondering about little Snow-in-the-Face and when we'd get to see him, and I said so.

Santa said, "He's still in the hospital. He'll be thrilled to death to see you boys. He's a great little boy."

He opened his cabin door to go out and lock the boathouse.

I looked at Poetry, and he looked at me, and we stared at each other.

Then Santa said, "Let's all go. We'll take a boat ride."

In a jiffy we were all outside, following Santa, walking in and along beside the white path his flashlight made.

"Well, what do you know!" Santa said all of a sudden, stopping and holding the light on the boathouse door. "I must have locked it after all and forgotten I did it."

We stopped while he shone the light on the Yale padlock on the door, and I saw it was locked.

Santa laughed. "Must be getting forgetful

in my old age." He turned, shot the flashlight all around, focusing it on the stumps out between us and the dock, then on the cottage and the chimney, and then on a hole in a hollow tree just above the boathouse.

And there, sitting in the hole, was a rust-red, blinking, long-eared screech owl, looking like an elderly woman sitting on the front porch of her house. Quick as a flash the owl spread its wings and flew like a shadow out into the night.

Poetry and I looked toward each other and sighed. We'd been fooled by our own imaginations, because if there's anything a girl sounds like when she is half crying in a high-pitched voice around Sugar Creek School, it is a screech owl, which makes a sort of moaning, wavering wail.

Well, that was that, and I felt very foolish.

All of us went to Santa's dock and climbed into his boat, taking his flashlight and also a bright electric lantern as you are supposed to do when you are out on a lake in a boat at night, so you won't run into some other boat and some other boat won't run into you. We roared across the dark water, around the neck of land, and then in a little while back toward camp.

Later, Poetry and Dragonfly and Circus and I went into our own tent. There was a small candle for a light on a folding table in one corner. It was as warm as toast in the tent in spite of its being really chilly outside, as it is most every night in Paul Bunyan country.

"What on earth is that water pail doing in the center of the tent?" I asked. It was right where I wanted to set my suitcase and open it.

"That's our stove," Circus said.

"Stove? That's a water pail!" Poetry exclaimed.

"That's where I want my suitcase," I said and started to move it.

But Circus yelled, "Don't touch it. You'll get burned. It's a stove!"

In the flickering light his monkey face looked ridiculous, and, knowing how mischievous he was, I said, "You're crazy." I started to take hold of the handle of the pail—and let go in a fierce hurry. The handle *was* hot, and there was a lot of heat coming from the outside of the pail and a whole lot coming from the inside!

It was pretty dark in the tent, so I carried the candle from the corner and looked in, and I wouldn't have believed it if I hadn't seen it, but there it was—one of the big round rocks Poetry and I had rolled into the fire a couple hours ago. It was still as hot as anything, and maybe it would stay hot nearly all night to keep us warm.

I crawled into my sleeping bag, and with Poetry in his right beside me, and Dragonfly and Circus on the other side of the tent in theirs, we were ready to try to stop talking and go to sleep.

Circus snuffed out the candle, and we all

were as quiet as we could be for a while, which wasn't very quiet. We could hear the rest of the gang—Big Jim and Tom Till and Little Jim and also Barry Boyland—still talking over in their tent maybe fifty feet away on the other side of the campfire.

In spite of having been scared by my own imagination, I was awfully sleepy, and I knew that in a minute I'd be gone. I was so sleepy I knew I wouldn't be able to say a very good good-night prayer to the heavenly Father. It is better for a boy to do most of his praying when he is wide awake, but I managed to say a few words, which I meant from the bottom of my heart, and they were that the little girl's parents would be brave even though their little girl had been kidnapped. I also prayed for Snow-in-the-Face and maybe a few other things.

Our gang hardly ever prayed together, because the boys were bashful about doing it, but each one of us nearly always prayed by himself. Once in a while, though, we did pray together when it was something extra-important and we thought maybe God wanted us to ask Him about it.

It certainly was a wonderful feeling—lying there in my cozy sleeping bag, warm as toast, listening to mosquitoes buzzing around my face. I had mosquito lotion on, though, even on my ears. All of us had been very careful, as the directions on the bottle said, not to get any on our lips or too near our eyes.

I certainly was glad I hadn't said I thought

anybody had been kidnapped and might be in Santa's boathouse. I didn't want to seem ridiculous to anybody except to Poetry and myself. But I wished I had been right, because, as my dad once said, nobody likes to believe he is wrong, even when he is.

I drifted away into a half dream, and it seemed I could hear the washing of the lake wavelets on the shore, and they were mixed up with Dragonfly's snoring. Also it seemed somebody was near me with a saw and was sawing wood, and the pile of sawdust was getting higher and higher until Poetry and I were standing ankle deep in it. I took off my shoes to get the sawdust out of them, and they were filled with green and white paint.

Then somebody started pounding and making a slapping noise, and I woke up. It was Dragonfly, twisting and turning in his sleep and slapping at his face and ears. So I asked him, "'S'matter?"

He answered back in a whining whisper and said, "These crazy mosquitoes are driving me wild. They are the biggest mosquitoes in the world!"

"Didn't you put on any repellent?"

And he said, "No, I'm allergic to it. It makes me sneeze!" Right that second he sneezed—twice.

I said, "You're probably allergic to mosquitoes too."

That woke Poetry up. He groaned a couple times and then really woke up and said, "Talk about big mosquitoes. Did you ever hear the story about the two mosquitoes who had a noisy argument?"

"It sounds like we're on the midway of a mosquito circus right now," Dragonfly said.

"I mean it," Poetry began. "There was a big argument between two mosquitoes who lived up here in the Chippewa Forest. One night the two of them were flying around looking for somebody to eat, and they found Dragonfly lying asleep out on the beach. So one of them said, 'Let's pick him up and fly him home and eat him *there*.' 'Naw,' the other one said, 'let's not. Let's eat him right here. If we take him home, the big ones will just take him away from us.'"

We made Dragonfly put on some lotion, and pretty soon he was asleep again. But now I was awake, thinking about the kidnapper.

Poetry nudged me and said, "Bill—*sh!*"

When I rolled over close to his face, he said, "I've got an idea."

Right away I was *wide* awake.

He said, "Remember the time I had a hunch back at Sugar Creek, and you and I got up and went out in the night, and the gang captured a robber digging for buried treasure down by the old sycamore tree?"

"Well?" I said.

And he said, "I've got that same kind of a hunch tonight. I still think that a screech owl wasn't what we heard. Why didn't we open the boathouse and look in?"

I wondered that myself, now that he mentioned it.

I heard Poetry zip a long zip on his sleeping bag, and all of a sudden my heart began to beat faster. I knew he and I were going to get up and go down to that boathouse and investigate.

There wouldn't be any real danger. If there *was* any little girl in there, we could probably hear her, and we could wake up Santa or Barry and the whole gang. And if there wasn't anything to our idea, then we still wouldn't seem ridiculous to anyone except ourselves.

8

I was glad a little wind was blowing so that the waves of the lake were washing against the shore, and also that Dragonfly snored. We wouldn't be heard if we kept real quiet.

Poetry and I put on our shoes, pants, and sweaters and worked our way out through the tent opening. Carrying our flashlights, we sneaked up along the beach toward Santa's cabin and his boathouse.

Suddenly I stopped. The whole idea seemed absolutely crazy. I said, "You don't think for a minute that any kidnapper would be dumb enough to hide out in a boathouse that wasn't any more than fifty yards from where somebody actually lived, do you?"

"Who said anything about any kidnapper hiding out?" Poetry said. "He's maybe a hundred miles away from here by now. But he could have left the Ostberg girl there, couldn't he?"

"Why—" I said.

He stopped me and hissed in my ear, "Not so loud!"

We'd been following a little footpath we knew about from having been there the year before. I was trembling, maybe because I was a little cold. But also I couldn't see any sense to

Poetry's thinking maybe the kidnapper had the Ostberg girl in that boathouse.

"You're scared!" Poetry accused, and I said I wasn't but only thought his idea was crazy.

"It *can't* be," Poetry said. "Listen . . ." Then he told me what he'd been thinking. "What if the kidnapper, who, as the paper said, is supposed to be a lumberman, was looking for an empty cabin somewhere up here to hide out in, and suppose he drove off onto a side road to dodge the police who might be looking for his car. And suppose he got off on the little half-hidden road that leads to Santa's cabin, which nobody hardly ever uses. And suppose he found the boathouse with the door open, and then just suppose that he put the girl in there, gagged her, and tied her up, like kidnappers do. And then suppose that while he was there, Santa and us boys came roaring up to the dock in the boat. Wouldn't the kidnapper be scared, and maybe lock the girl in, and beat it himself, and—"

Well, it made a little sense, so I hurried along behind Poetry, my heart beating faster still because we were hurrying so fast. Pretty soon, when we were almost there, he stopped all of a sudden and said, "*Sh!*"

I was quiet because I'd heard a sound as plain as day myself. It was a car engine running somewhere. It sounded as if it was at the top of the hill above the boathouse. We knew there was a sandy road up there, because we'd been on it once ourselves.

"Somebody's stuck in the sand," Poetry said.

And it sure sounded like it. The engine was whirring and whirring. I'd seen cars stuck in sand and snow before, and I could imagine the driver, whoever he was, doing what is called "rocking" the car, starting and shifting from first gear to reverse and back and forth, and the wheels spinning, and still the car not getting out of the sand.

We were close to the boathouse now. Poetry aimed his beam of light toward the door, and we both let out excited gasps. The boathouse door was wide open, and the hinge of the lock was hanging as though somebody had forced it open with a crowbar.

We flashed our lights around inside. Nobody was there, but a cot at the other end was messed up as if somebody had been lying on it. A pile of shavings was on the floor, and sawdust was scattered around under a carpenter's workbench. On the wall above the workbench were a lot of tools such as screwdrivers, saws, and planes. Maybe Santa had been working there, making something during the day.

"Quick!" Poetry ordered. "Let's go up the hill and get his license number."

I wanted to tell Santa or Barry or *somebody* and get a lot of noisy action, but I knew Poetry was right. Maybe we were already too late, and maybe we couldn't do anything helpful. We'd probably be shot if we were seen by the man, whoever he was. But if we could get the license

number, it might help the police to trail him—
if he really was the kidnapper.

Up that hill we went, following the hardly-
ever-used road. At the top we turned right and
slipped along the edge of Santa's woods, where
we could barely see the path ahead. But we
knew it would come out at the sandy road a little later, which it did.

We could see, even with our flashlights off,
which they had to be, that it was a new car. We
sneaked up behind it. It had its taillights and
parking lights on, and the driver was starting
slowly, going forward a few feet, then back-
ward, then forward, but not getting anywhere.

Already I was almost close enough to see
the license plate, but I didn't dare turn on my
flashlight, or the guy would find out we were
there.

"Wait," Poetry said, "I'll sneak up behind
that tree." He started to go, then he whispered
to me, "Down, Bill! Quick!"

Down we ducked and didn't dare make a
sound, because the car engine had stopped
and the guy was opening his door and getting
out. He made a dive for the back left wheel,
and we heard him mumbling something that
sounded like mad swear words.

I was glad that Little Jim wasn't there. It always
hurts him to hear anybody swear, because the
One whose name is used in such a terrible way
when a person swears is Little Jim's Best
Friend. I was glad he wasn't there for another
reason too, and that was that when he hears

somebody using filthy rotten words like that, he can't stand it and sometimes calls right out and says, "Stop swearing!"

We certainly didn't want anybody to call out to that man in the automobile.

"What's he doing?" I whispered in Poetry's ear and didn't need to ask, because I heard a hissing noise coming from that left back tire.

"The crazy goof!" I said to Poetry. "He's letting air out of his tire!"

Sssssss . . .

It made me feel creepy, because if a man who wanted to get away quick was foolish enough to let air out of his tires, he must be insane.

In a minute the tire had stopped hissing, and the guy, still grunting and mumbling to himself as if he was terribly mad and also maybe a little scared, was down on his knees beside the other back tire. Right away there was another hissing noise.

Then the man stood up and made a dive for the front seat and started to rock the car again. He backed up, and started forward, and the wheels started spinning and—

"Hey!" Poetry and I said at the same time. "The car is moving! He's getting away!"

He turned his flashlight on the back of the car to get the number, and it was a Minnesota plate. My mind took a picture of it quick, and I knew I'd never forget the number, but just to make sure, I kept saying it to myself, over and over and over.

The second that new black car was out of that sandy place, it shot down the road like a bullet.

And there wasn't a thing we could do. *Not a thing,* I thought, and wondered if the girl might be in the backseat and why on earth hadn't we tried to rescue her if she was there?

We ran to the place where the car had been stuck and studied the road. Poetry let out a gasp and said, "He's awfully smart, that guy. Look at these tire tracks, will you?"

I looked, and Poetry was right. First I looked at how narrow they had been before they got stuck in the sand. Then I looked at them *after* they'd gone on up the road, and they were almost half again as wide.

"Letting out that air increased traction!" Poetry said. "But he can't run on them half flat very far or very fast. He'll have to stop at the first gas station and get some air. Come on! Let's get to a telephone quick and call the Bemidji and the Pass Lake police and have all the gas stations watch for him. Give them the license number, and I'll bet the police will catch him!"

With that, Poetry whirled around, his flashlight in his hand, and we were starting to run up the sandy lane to where the fire warden lived, when I noticed something shining in the grass at the side of the road.

"Shine your light over here a minute," I said.

I stooped over to pick up whatever it was,

thinking it might be something the kidnapped girl might have had, but, shucks, it was only a piece of glass. I picked it up, though, and was going to throw it away when Poetry grabbed my arm and stopped me and said, "Wait! Let me see it!"

"It's a piece of broken glass," I said, but I let him look at it up close with his flashlight.

"Sure," he said, "it's a clue."

"How could a piece of broken glass be a clue?"

"'Cause it isn't stained with weather or anything, which means it hasn't been lying out here very long," he said and tucked it in his pocket.

It wasn't any time to argue, but I thought his detective ideas were nearly all imagination.

He was running awfully fast for a barrel-shaped boy, and I was having a hard time keeping up with him as we raced along. We knew the fire warden didn't live very far up that sandy lane—we had been there the year before and knew that his house was the nearest one that had a telephone. Santa didn't have one in his cabin because he didn't want his vacation spoiled by people calling him up. If he needed a telephone, he could always go to where there was one, he said.

"Slow down," I said to Poetry all of a sudden. "Maybe we're on a wild-goose chase. Maybe we're crazy to waste a lot of good sleeping time chasing an imaginary kidnapper. How do we know that was a kidnapper's car? What if it was just *anybody* who got stuck in the sand? He wouldn't appreciate having policemen stop him and ask a lot of questions!"

"It wasn't just *anybody!*" Poetry said. "That guy was down there in the boathouse less than a half hour ago, and there was a girl there too. See?"

He stopped long enough to pull out of his pocket something *he* had picked up back there where the car had been, and it was a girl's yellow scarf!

"But that could be any woman's or any girl's scarf," I said.

"It could *not,*" Poetry disagreed with me with a very sure voice and also an excited one. "See that green paint on it—and look! Here's some white paint too."

Well, I remembered Santa had been using green and white paint inside the boathouse that very afternoon, and remembering that put wings on my feet. I ran like a deer up that winding sandy road toward the fire warden's house and a telephone.

9

If people had seen Poetry and me galloping down that narrow winding road, following the bobbing path of our flashlights, our breath coming in quick pants, they might have thought we were crazy. It was one of the crookedest roads I'd ever seen in my life, and—would you believe it?—Poetry couldn't resist puffing a part of a poem as we raced along toward the fire warden's cabin. The poem started out like this:

> "There was a crooked man
> Who walked a crooked mile;
> He found a crooked sixpence
> Beside a crooked stile—"

We didn't find any sixpence, but we did find something else, and in a minute I'll tell you what it was.

Well, I knew we were ready to turn the last bend in the road just before we got to the fire warden's house, when Poetry suddenly stopped running. He flashed his light down the road ahead of us, where, as plain as day, I saw a big beautiful reddish-brown deer standing right in the center of the road. Its head was up, and its antlers looked very pretty. Its ears were large and were spread out the way our old brindle cow back home spreads hers out when she is interested in something or scared. That deer was *really* scared. It turned, and like a reddish-brown flash it was gone, leaping away and disappearing into the trees at the side of the road.

It's a good thing we saw the deer, though. If we hadn't, maybe we wouldn't have stopped and wouldn't have heard what we heard right that second. We both heard it at the same time, and it sounded exactly like what we'd heard before when we were standing out by the woodpile.

"It's another screech owl," Poetry said and started on.

I stopped him and said, "Maybe it's a loon."

"It's coming from out there in the trees," he said. "Loons don't stay up here in the woods. They're out on the lake or else right close to it all the time."

We both listened, while my heart thumped like Dad's hammer driving a terribly big nail into a log in our barn at Sugar Creek. The cry certainly sounded exactly like what we'd heard at the boathouse. I remembered the simple-looking owl we'd seen sitting in the hole of the hollow tree and how it had flown away, but this time I just *knew* it wasn't any owl or any loon.

"Let's go see," Poetry said.

I said, "What if it's the girl? What'll we do? What'll—"

"Let's decide later," Poetry interrupted me.

We flashed our lights out toward the trees

and couldn't see a thing, but we heard again that eerie cry that was like a loon being choked, and we started toward it. Our lights shoved back the dark as we went along, walking in their yellowish bobbing paths.

We crept up slowly. I had a big stick in one hand, ready to use it as a club if I had to. For some reason we didn't stop to think that maybe we ought to get to the fire warden's house *first* and tell him. Instead we just kept right on going, the pine needles on the ground making a spooky noise under our shoes.

Then Poetry stopped, and I, who had been following, bumped into him.

"Look! There's a blanket with somebody wrapped up in it!"

It was a blanket of many colors, the kind almost all the families in Sugar Creek have in their homes.

Then I heard a low, half-muffled half cry again, and we knew we'd found the kidnapped Ostberg girl.

Well, when I looked down at that blanket with the little five-year-old girl wrapped in it, and saw the handkerchief the kidnapper had stuffed into her mouth to keep her from talking or screaming, and as we unwrapped her and saw that her hands and feet were tied together, and when I saw the pretty yellow all-tangled-up hair around her face and shoulders, I forgot all about having been half scared to death a while ago. Instead, I got a terribly angry feeling inside that made me want to find the kidnapper and for just about three minutes turn loose both of my fiery-tempered fists on his chin and nose and stomach and knock the living daylights out of him.

My dad had told me true stories about how there are crazy or wicked men in the world who don't have any respect for God or other people —and how every one of them ought to be locked up somewhere until a doctor can cure them, or else they should stay in jail for life or be executed for their awful crimes. Anyway, there ought not to be even one of them allowed to run free in this world, and if they are allowed to, it's the law's fault or the people's fault.

Well, we couldn't stand there just staring and wasting good temper on something we couldn't help. We had to get the fire warden quickly, and he would know what to do.

Poetry certainly had presence of mind. "Take my flashlight," he ordered. Almost before I could get it into my hand, he was stooped over and taking the gag out of the girl's mouth and with his pocketknife was cutting the cords that were around her wrists and ankles.

It was pitiful the way that little girl, who was only three or four years younger than Little Jim, sobbed when we got the handkerchief out of her mouth. She had a terribly scared look on her face. "Help!" she half cried but in a very muffled hoarse voice, as if she had been crying for a long time and had worn her vocal cords out.

"Mama! Mama!" she cried. "I want my m-m-mama!" Then she would just go into hysterical sobbing, and we couldn't understand a word she was saying.

"We're your friends," we tried to tell her. "We've come to rescue you. We'll help you get to the fire warden's house and—"

But the poor little thing was so scared that she couldn't say a word we could understand, except that she wanted her mama. She was also so weak she couldn't stand up and wouldn't be able to walk the rest of the way to the fire warden's house, and we didn't think we ought to try to carry her.

We had to do something quick, though, because she probably needed a doctor, so Poetry made me go on the run for the fire warden, while he stayed with the helpless girl. He would yell to us when we came back, he said, and flash his light so we would know where he and the girl were.

I tell you, I ran, but I was trembling so much that it was hard for me to keep going.

Soon I came in sight of some white birch saplings that crisscrossed each other, making a homemade gate. I could see a house just beyond and an old unpainted barn. Also there was a light in the window of what looked like an ordinary bungalow, which meant that maybe the fire warden hadn't gone to bed yet.

I lay down and squeezed myself under the gate and in a minute was knocking at the door of the bungalow.

"Quick!" I panted as soon as the door opened. "We've found the kidnapped Ostberg girl! She's out there in the trees wrapped up in a blanket and—" Right that second, I remembered about the car and its license number. I half yelled the things I wanted to say.

The fire warden looked ridiculous in his green-striped pajamas as he stood in the doorway of his kitchen with a flashlight in his hand.

"What is it?" a woman's voice called from somewhere back in the house. It was probably the voice of his sleepy wife, who had just woke up and wanted to know what was going on.

"Quick!" I said. "The license number is—" I told him "—and he's got two half-flat tires and will have to stop somewhere at a gas station and get some air."

I guess maybe the fire warden must have known all about the Ostberg girl having been kidnapped, because it only took me a little while to explain enough to him so that he was ready for action. He was kind of an old man, but he was very spry and could think fast. While his wife was dressing somewhere in the house, he made two quick phone calls, and almost right away he got out his powerful electric lantern, and the three of us were on our way to his homemade gate.

There he flashed his light around a little and said, "Well, what do you know—he must have thought our driveway was another bend in the road. He started to turn in, then swung out again. See?"

I used my own flashlight on the tire tracks and saw, as plain as day, that some car *had* made a sharp turn there. And as sure as the nose on Dragonfly's face, which, as you maybe know, turns south at the end, I noticed that the back tires had wider patterns than the front.

We hurried up to where Poetry was waiting for us with the kidnapped girl. The little girl was still so scared that she couldn't talk without great sobs getting mixed up with her words, and you couldn't understand her very well. But the fire warden's wife just knelt down on the ground beside that tangled-up-golden-haired girl, gathered her into her arms, and crooned to her as if she was her very own little girl. Then she stood up and, being a very strong woman, wouldn't let her husband carry the girl but carried her herself and crooned to her all the way back to their house.

When we first got to where Poetry was, I'd noticed he was standing with his New Testament in one hand, shining his flashlight on its pages and reading something.

What on earth? I thought and waited for a chance to ask him what he was doing and why.

On the way to the fire warden's house, while I was wishing the rest of the gang was there and thinking that we'd have some wonderful stories to tell that would be even better than Paul Bunyan stories, and also that we could tell our folks the same ones, I said to Poetry, "What were you doing back there—reading stories to her to keep her quiet?"

"No, I was looking at some Bible verses," he said. "I'll tell you tomorrow—or later, anyway."

Well, I've got to step on the gas with this story. We came to the birch sapling gate, and there we stood while I showed Poetry where the kidnapper had started to turn in and then made a sharp turn and gone on. Poetry held his flashlight down close to the ground and studied the patterns of the tracks and said, "He must have slowed down a lot right here, or the tire patterns wouldn't be so plain."

Then we saw the headlights—and also a spotlight—of a car swinging down the road toward us real fast.

"It's the police already," the fire warden said, and it was.

There was certainly some excitement around there and also inside of me for a while.

First, they made sure the girl was all right. In fact, Mrs. Fire Warden sat in the backseat of their car with the girl in her arms, and the girl was asleep. In another few minutes an ambulance was coming to take her to a hospital.

"How'd you get here so quick?" Poetry asked one of the big blue-uniformed policemen.

He answered in a pleasant voice, as though he thought a boy's questions were as important as a grown-up's. "We were only a few miles up the highway when the call came through on the radio, and so here we are!"

Even before he had finished saying what he was saying, I was thinking how absolutely silly it is for anybody to think he can commit a crime and not get caught and punished sooner or later, even though they might not have caught the kidnapper yet.

In the next seventeen minutes I saw one of the most interesting things I'd ever seen, and it made me even more sure that anybody—man or boy or woman or girl—was just plumb crazy to try to be smarter than the law is and get by with any kind of a crime or sin.

I whispered it to Poetry when I saw what the policemen were doing, saying, "Nobody can get by with any kind of crime," and Poetry, who is almost as good a Christian as Little Jim is, and who not only has a lot of poems on the tip of his tongue ready to be quoted any second but also knows many Bible verses, quoted one of them to me right that minute instead of a poem: "I was reading, 'Do not be deceived, God is not mocked; for whatever a man sows, this he will also reap.'" He added to it another, which was, "It is appointed for men to die once and after this comes judgment."

One of the cops heard him and looked up from what he was doing. "That's right, son. That's what my mother used to say."

Then we quit talking and in the light of the spotlight from the police car watched what was going on.

What in the world? I thought when I saw one officer take what looked like a fishing tackle box out of his car, carry it to the gate, and set it down. Then he went back to the car and brought out something else.

"What's that?" Poetry wanted to know.

And the friendly cop said, "A flashbulb camera with a reversible tripod. We're going to snap a picture of these tire tracks."

Why? I thought but didn't want to seem dumb enough to ask because I supposed Poetry knew.

First, the officer laid a black cardboard down alongside the tire track, the edge of the cardboard looking like a ruler with little white inch-marks on it. Then he set up his camera with its lens focused on the track. As quick as a wink there was a blinding flash of light.

Then he opened the kit that looked like a fishing tackle box and took out a spray can, like the kind Mom uses on flies and bugs and stuff in our garden. He began to spray something very carefully all over about two feet of the track.

"It's shellac," the policeman said.

I said, "Why?"

And he said, "Wait and see," which I had to do.

Pretty soon he stopped spraying, screwed off the container at the bottom of the spraying device, and screwed on a can of something else and started in doing the same thing, pumping away very carefully, not letting the spray strike very hard on the sandy tracks, so as not to make any of the sand move.

I looked at the other things in the kit,

which was spread wide open in front of us. I saw what looked like a large salt shaker like the one Mom uses when she is cooking raw fried potatoes. Also there was a rubber cup, two other containers, a spoon and a spatula that looked like the long flat stick our doctor uses when he looks into my throat and makes me say, "Ah."

"The shellac makes the tire impression firm enough to stand the weight of the plaster of paris without crumbling it," the officer said.

And even though I didn't understand what it was all about or why, it was very interesting to watch. Right away they started getting the plaster of paris ready. They mixed some in the rubber cup, doing it almost exactly the way I had seen our Sugar Creek dentist do it, and also the way we do it in school when we make an art plaque. The only difference was that they sprinkled in a little salt to make it harden quicker. The plaster of paris was poured on top of the water and allowed to sink to the bottom of the rubber cup until the water couldn't take any more. Then it was stirred with a spoon and very carefully dipped out into the tire impressions.

"What's he doing now?" I asked Poetry, when some sticks and twigs and little pieces of string were laid on top of the first layer of plaster of paris.

"I don't know," Poetry said. "Reinforcing it, maybe," which, it turned out, the officer was doing. Right away they put on another, thicker, layer of plaster of paris, and then it was ready to let harden.

After a while, when the officers were sure it was solid, they would just lift it up, and there would be a perfect plaster cast, a foot and a half long, of the tire marks, which, whenever they found the kidnapper's car, would help them prove that he was really guilty.

We couldn't stay there all night, though, because tomorrow the gang had a lot of things to do and see. And besides, when a boy wants to be in good health, he has to have plenty of sleep at night, so the fire warden decided to drive us back to camp while the police looked around for other clues. We gave them the piece of glass and the yellow scarf with the paint on it and went with the fire warden back to camp to try to get some sleep, even though we were still excited. Boy, oh, boy, it had been a great experience!

About an hour later, after waking up all the gang and telling them the news, we were in our tent again ready to sleep. The big hot round rock in the pail in the center of the tent certainly had helped keep the place warm.

When I was in my sleeping bag again, as warm as toast, I felt that I had really done something important in life. I got to thinking about that little kidnapped girl, knowing how glad her parents would feel when they got the news, which they might have already. Maybe they were already on their way up here to see her. Of course, if she was really sick or had been mistreated terribly by the kidnapper, she might have to be in the hospital quite a while.

For a few minutes just before I dropped off, I was listening to the waves lapping against our sandy shore and was thinking and thinking and thinking. I knew that if I had been standing by the shore looking out on the moonlit water, the rolling waves might look just like our oats field does down along Sugar Creek when the wind is blowing, waving and waving and rolling and rolling and rolling and looking very wonderful. And for a minute I could see my dad sitting up on our big tractor, driving along and maybe singing a song that nearly always, when Dad sang or whistled, was a hymn we used in our church. It might be the one that goes:

> Bringing in the sheaves,
> Bringing in the sheaves,
> We shall come rejoicing
> Bringing in the sheaves.

Then I remembered Poetry's Bible verse: "Whatever a man sows, this he will also reap." It was absolutely silly, I thought again, for anybody to sow a lot of sin in his life and not expect to reap a harvest of the same kind. The verse also said God couldn't be mocked, which might mean that every man would surely be punished for living a sinful life.

Then I imagined different things, such as Dad saying to Mom, "I wonder how Bill is getting along up North," and Mom saying, "Oh, nine—I hope. I wonder if he is warm enough. It gets so cold up there at night, and you know how he is—he kicks the covers off in his sleep and lies there and half freezes without even waking up." And Dad would remember that I had my sleeping bag, and Mom would sigh, and they'd go to sleep. They really were wonderful parents, I thought.

And the waves of the blue-water lake rolled and rolled and tossed around some, and then a great big pair of horns stuck themselves up out of the lake, and then a cow's face, and then a whole cow splashed and splashed, and the water turned blue all around the big blue cow. And Mom tried to stop him from swishing around so much because he was splashing around in her washing machine and getting too much bluing on her clothes.

And then I must have dropped off to sleep, because the next thing I knew it was morning, and the gang was making a lot of boys' noise. And we had another wonderful day ahead in which to live and have new adventures.

Well, here I am, with all the pages filled up and not even room to tell you about how the kidnapper got away from the police and how the Sugar Creek Gang ran *ker-smack* onto his trail all by themselves the very next day, and what a fierce fight we had and everything.

But just as quick as I can, I'll get going on that exciting story, which was maybe the most exciting experience that ever happened to us. Maybe I'll get started writing tomorrow.